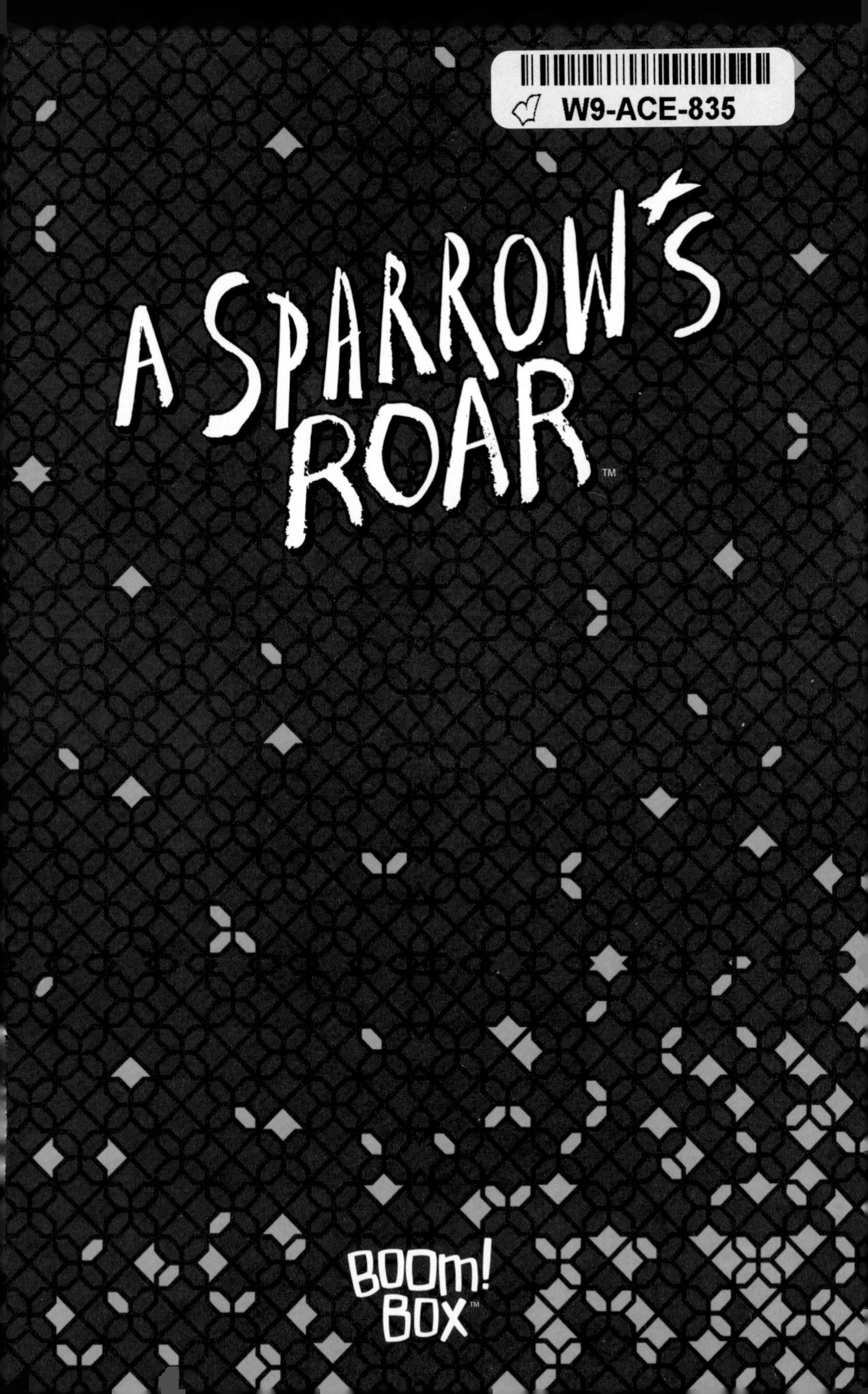
W9-ACE-835
A SPARROW'S ROAR™
BOOM! BOX™

BOOM! BOX™

A SPARROW'S ROAR, October 2019. Published by BOOM! Box, a division of Boom Entertainment, Inc.

For information regarding the CPSIA on this printed material, call: (203) 595-3636 and provide reference #RICH – 865879.

BOOM! Studios, 5670 Wilshire Boulevard, Suite 400, Los Angeles, CA 90036-5679. Printed in USA. First Printing.

ISBN: 978-1-68415-476-0, eISBN: 978-1-64144-615-0

A SPARROW'S ROAR™

CREATED & WRITTEN BY

C.R. CHUA & PAOLO CHIKIAMCO

ILLUSTRATED BY

C.R. CHUA

COVER BY

C.R. CHUA

DESIGNER
JILLIAN CRAB

ASSISTANT EDITOR
MICHAEL MOCCIO

EDITOR
SHANNON WATTERS

CHAPTER ONE

HOW COULD A NIGHT SO BRIGHT...
...SCAR MY SOUL WITH SUCH DARKNESS?

MAKE WAY!
MAKE WAY!

IS THAT--?
CAN'T BE!
--SHE HELD THE MOUNTAIN PASS FOR TWO WEEKS WITHOUT ANY AID--
I HEARD SHE ONCE DEFEATED NINETEEN MEN ALONE--
BUT WHY WOULD SHE BE HERE ALREADY?
I TOLD YOU! IT *IS* HER!
WE'RE GOING TO BE LATE FOR--UGH!
C'MON, THERE'S NO WAY YOU CAN BE SURE IT'S HER!
"LOOK AT THE LION, SIS! OF *COURSE* IT'S HER!"
"LOOKS MORE LIKE A BIRD TO ME..."
"SIS! YOU KNOW THE STORIES!"
C'MON C'MON! WE GOTTA GET CLOSER!
HEY, DON'T PUSH THE--

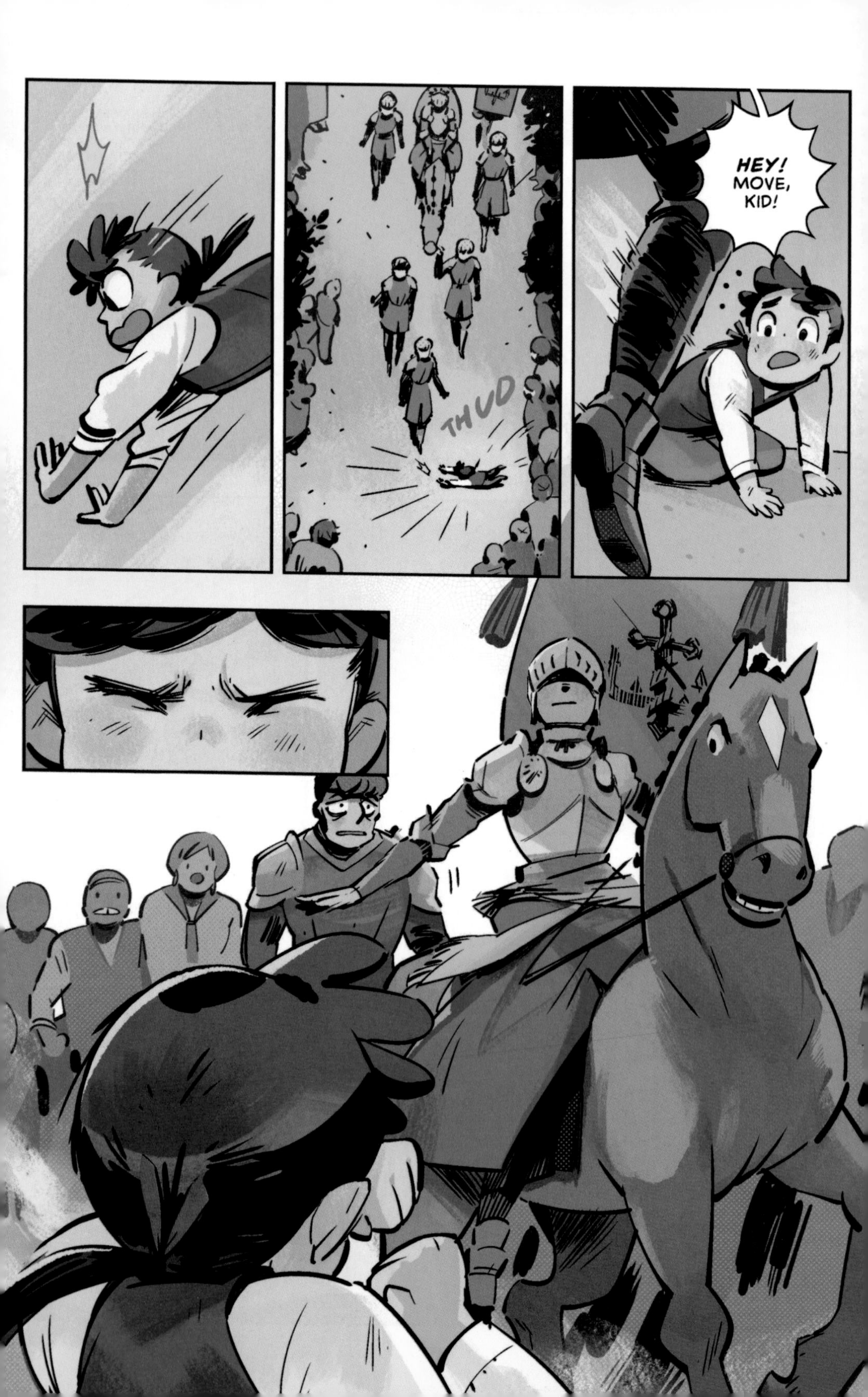
THUD
HEY! MOVE, KID!

TH-THANK YOU...
I-I'M SO, SO SORRY, YOUR HONOR! I TRIED TO KEEP HIM UNDER CONTROL, BUT HE WAS JUST SO EXCITED AND--
T-THANK YOU!
OOOOH! WHY DON'T YOU LISTEN?
BOK
EVERYTHING IS WRONG.
GENERAL ELENA? IS ANYTHING WRONG?

BEFORE THEY BECAME A PART OF UNITY, THEY SAY ESTERPIKE'S FOUNDERS ONCE REFUSED TO SERVE A CORRUPT KING.
THEY WERE GIVEN A COWARD'S BRAND--THE MARK OF A SPARROW--AND EXILED.
"NO LAND SHALL GRANT YOU PEACE," SAID THE KING.
AND THE FOUNDERS' REPLY?
"PEACE IS EARNED, NOT GRANTED."
ESTERPIKE'S PEOPLE WERE WELL KNOWN FOR THEIR WANDERINGS--
--AND THEIR WARRIORS.
THEY HAVEN'T WANDERED FOR A WHILE NOW.

BUT THEY HAVE WARRIORS APLENTY.
KEEP YOUR ARM STRAIGHT!

NO, NO!
TWACK
AIM BEFORE YOU DRAW! DON'T JUST--

COME ON, PER! FOCUS!
I AM FOCUSED, 'LENA!

IF YOU WERE FOCUSED, WE WOULDN'T HAVE A BRAND NEW ARROW GARDEN.

MAYBE WE CAN TRY... ANOTHER STYLE. THERE ARE GREAT ARCHERS THAT DON'T CALL ESTERPIKE HOME.

THE NATION OF MARIAE, WHICH TOOK IN THE PEOPLE OF ESTERPIKE, IS PART OF AN ALLIANCE OF NATION-STATES APTLY CALLED UNITY.
BUT I'M FROM--
JUST PAY ATTENTION, PLEASE?
THE LONGBOWS OF MARIAE HAVE SERVED ITS LEGIONS FOR CENTURIES.
THEY REQUIRE STRENGTH, BUT YOU'VE NEVER LACKED IN THAT.
STRAKTON, A NATION OF SEAFARERS, PROVIDES THE NAVAL MIGHT OF THE ALLIANCE.
YOU COULD HANDLE A STRAKTON BOW, TOO, BUT YOU NEED TO HEED YOUR THREE PARALLELS AT ALL TIMES.

ETHERN, THE OLDEST NATION IN UNITY, IS HOME TO MOST OF ITS AGRICULTURAL WEALTH.
OF COURSE, FOR MOUNTED BATTLE, NOTHING BEATS AN ETHERN HORSE BOW, BUT YOU'LL NEED PRECISE SHOOTING AGAINST ARMORED FOES.
CAMBRIA, ONCE RENOWNED AS A HOME FOR LEARNING, IS NOW INFAMOUS INSTEAD FOR ITS FAILED REVOLT.
THE CAMBRIANS DON'T HAVE MUCH USE FOR ARCHERY, RELYING INSTEAD ON THEIR ARTIFICES.
MOST OF THEM ARE FORBIDDEN NOW...
...BUT I CAN SEE WHAT THEY HAVE AT THE CAPITAL IF YOU WANT TO BE--

AHHHH!
--UNCON-
VENTIONAL...
TWAK
TWAK
WOW, BABY
SPARROW--
--YOU TAKE TO
THE BOW AS WELL
AS YOUR SISTER
TAKES TO WINE.
AMELIA.
THE
DELEGATION
FROM THE
COUNCIL HAS
ARRIVED,
COMMANDER.
LET ME CHANGE,
AND I'LL MEET
YOU THERE.
GRRR...
THAT MEANS
YOU TOO.

ON BEHALF OF ESTERPIKE, I WELCOME THE REPRESENTATIVES OF OUR PARTNERS IN UNITY.
LADY ELENA, WE THANK YOU FOR YOUR GRACIOUS RECEPTION.
IT'S COMMANDER ELENA.
AND AFTER TOMORROW, GENERAL ELENA.
I DON'T KNOW WHY I CAN'T BE IN ARMOR, TOO...
BECAUSE THE ARMOR IS FOR LIONS, NOT FOR NOISY BABY SPARROWS.
BUT-!
HUSH.
GENERAL NILS WISHES TO WELCOME YOU TO THE COUNCIL WITH A MODEST GIFT--
"AN AGED RELIC FOUND ON THE COAST OF STRACKTON, THE OLDEST OBJECT KNOWN BEARING THE PROUD STAMP OF THE LIONS.
"MAYHAP THIS COULD BE A CLUE TO UNRAVELLING THE GLORIOUS HISTORY OF--"

WHY LOOK SO FAR IN THE PAST FOR GLORY?
WHEN COMMANDER ELENA'S OWN DEEDS ARE YET SO FRESH?
WHAT'S WITH THE GRAND-STANDING?
OOOH
ROLL
ROLL
DON'T YOU EVER LISTEN AT BRIEFINGS?
WHY? MEETINGS ARE BORING.
AND I'M NOT A LION YET, AFTER ALL.
"UNITY'S SUPPOSED TO BE RULED BY A GRAND GENERAL.
"CHOSEN BY AT LEAST THREE OF THE FOUR COUNCIL GENERALS.
"THING IS, THERE HASN'T BEEN A FULL FOUR GENERALS IN FIVE YEARS, NOT SINCE MARTA DIED--"

--IN THE GREAT ASH REBELLION, WHERE YOU, COMMANDER ELENA, TOOK UP THE FALLEN GENERAL'S BOW AND RALLIED THE LIONS TO VICTORY AGAINST--
"--THE CAMBRIAN SECESSIONISTS, PREVENTING THEM FROM COMPLETING THEIR MAD MARCH ON OUR UNDEFENDED CAPITAL."
COMMANDER ELENA, GENERAL FERRIS IS CERTAIN YOU'LL BE PLEASED BY HOW OUR CAMBRIAN WEAVERS--
HA HA HA!

HA!
HA!
WILL. YOU. STOP. YOUR. CHORTLING?!
OH, BUT IT'S SO AMUSING HOW YOUR GENERALS SEEM SO SURE YOU KNOW WHAT THE COMMANDER WOULD WANT, WHEN NONE EVEN BOTHERED ASKING HER?
HA
HA
WIPE
COMMANDER ELENA! YOU HAVE ASKED AND GENERAL LAKME HAS PROVIDED!
WAIT.
I NEVER--
THE FINEST COLLECTION OF FIREWORKS IN THE THREE NATIONS!
YEEEEEESSS!
AMELIA, WILL YOU SEE TO OUR GUESTS FOR A MOMENT?
I BELIEVE SOMETHING REQUIRES MY... ATTENTION.
OOPS

DO YOU UNDERSTAND HOW IRRESPONSIBLE IT IS TO FORGE A LETTER FROM ME?!
BUT... FIREWORKS! YOU LOVE THEM, ELENA, DON'T LIE!
THAT'S NOT THE... ARRGH!
THESE GENERALS... DO YOU KNOW HOW HARD IT'S GOING TO BE FOR ME TO EARN THEIR RESPECT?
IF THEY DIDN'T RESPECT YOU, THEY WOULDN'T MAKE YOU A GENERAL!
IT'S MORE COMPLICATED THAN THAT. AFTER THE REBELLION, THE PUBLIC EXPECTS...
LOOK, THEY'RE NOT GOING TO TAKE AN EIGHTEEN YEAR OLD SERIOUSLY!
ESPECIALLY NOT ONE THAT ASKS THEM FOR *FIREWORKS* FOR HER BIRTHDAY!
OKAY! OKAY, I GET IT.

GO ON, THEN. POLISH YOUR FANCY ARMOR FOR THE FEAST. I'LL MAKE YOUR TEA.
PER...
HEY, I'M SURE YOU'LL HAVE ATTENDANTS AND STUFF AT THE CAPITAL, RIGHT? SO...LET ME TAKE CARE OF YOU ONCE MORE, FOR OLD TIME'S SAKE?
PER...
DON'T FORGET THE--
HONEY! YES, I KNOW!
Vita
ETHER
I'VE GOT JUST THE THING...

"NEIGHBORS OF ESTERPIKE...
"...PROUD LIONS, AND NOBLE GUESTS..."
THOUGH MY TITLE MAY CHANGE, AND MY DUTIES TAKE ME FARTHER AFIELD...
KNOW THAT MY DESIRE TO SERVE YOU REMAINS EVER STEADFAST.
"I MAY HAVE COME OF AGE, BUT I WILL ALWAYS COME HOME."
AFTER ALL **NO ONE**--
--CELEBRATES QUITE **LIKE US**.

LET'S GET...
...THIS PARTY...
...STARTED!

FWIP
FWIP
ELENA!
--SOMEONE'S SHOOTING--!
FIRE--!
--UNDER ATTACK!--
ELE--
--NA!
GENERAL ELENA!

UM...WE'RE HERE, YOUR HONOR. THE COUNCIL IS NOT YET COMPLETE.
BUT I EXPECT YOU'D LIKE TO MAKE YOUR REPORT REGARDLESS?
AH!
YES.

OH, MY DEAR ELENA.
WE'LL GET THOSE BASTARDS!
!

ESTERPIKE MAY NOT BE OUR BIGGEST CONCERN AT THE MOMENT.
STRAKTON! HOW CAN YOU SAY THAT? HER SISTER IS DEAD!
AND OUR RESPONSIBILITY IS TO THE LIVING.
THINK!
WHY WOULD THE CAMBRIANS ATTACK ESTERPIKE, RATHER THAN COME STRAIGHT THROUGH THE TARID PASS?
BECAUSE IT WAS ELENA AND THE LIONS THAT STOPPED THEM THE LAST TIME THEY TRIED THAT!
WHICH IS WHY IT'S LIKELY THEY SENT A SMALL FORCE TO CRIPPLE THE LIONS, BEFORE MARCHING THEIR MAIN ARMY THROUGH THE PASS.
"I SHOULD SAY SOMETHING."

LAKME OF ETHERN
AND NILS OF STRAKTON.
LEGENDS AND LEADERS.
THEY DEBATE ESTERPIKE'S
FATE AS IF I'M NOT HERE.
AND, WELL, IN
A WAY, I'M NOT.
BUT I DIDN'T COME
ALL THIS WAY TO BE
STONEWALLED.
YOUR HONORS,
I WILL NOT ACCEPT--
SLAM
I CAME FOR AID.
I CAME FOR--
SORRY
I'M LATE!

GIVEN THE CIRCUMSTANCES, I SENT MY COURIERS TO CAMBRIA FOR INFORMATION.
ANOTHER REBELLION WILL BE DEVASTATING FOR ALL, BUT FOR US CAMBRIANS ESPECIALLY.
YOU...
GENERAL ELENA, MY DEEPEST CONDOLENCES--
--LET ME BE FIRST TO ASSURE YOU THAT--

FWIP
FWIP
ELENA!
WHAT ARE YOUR ORDERS?
THEIR LEADER...
...IF I CAN STOP HIM...

"THERE!"
ELENA!

TWANNNNNG
...
...
...
OF ALL THE GODFORSAKEN--!

THROW
USE THE DAMNED SWORD!

WHERE IS THE COMMANDER?!
I LEFT HER AT HO--
--LOOK OUT!

TWACK
ELENA!
THAT'S MORE LIKE IT.

YIELD, CAMBRIAN!
NEVER AGAIN. NO SURRENDER.
NOT FROM US.

KLK
FWOooo OoM
tsck
NOT FROM YOU.

I'LL...
--GIVE YOU MY PERSONAL ASSURANCE--
--THAT THE CAMBRIAN GOVERNMENT WILL--

I'LL KILL YOU!

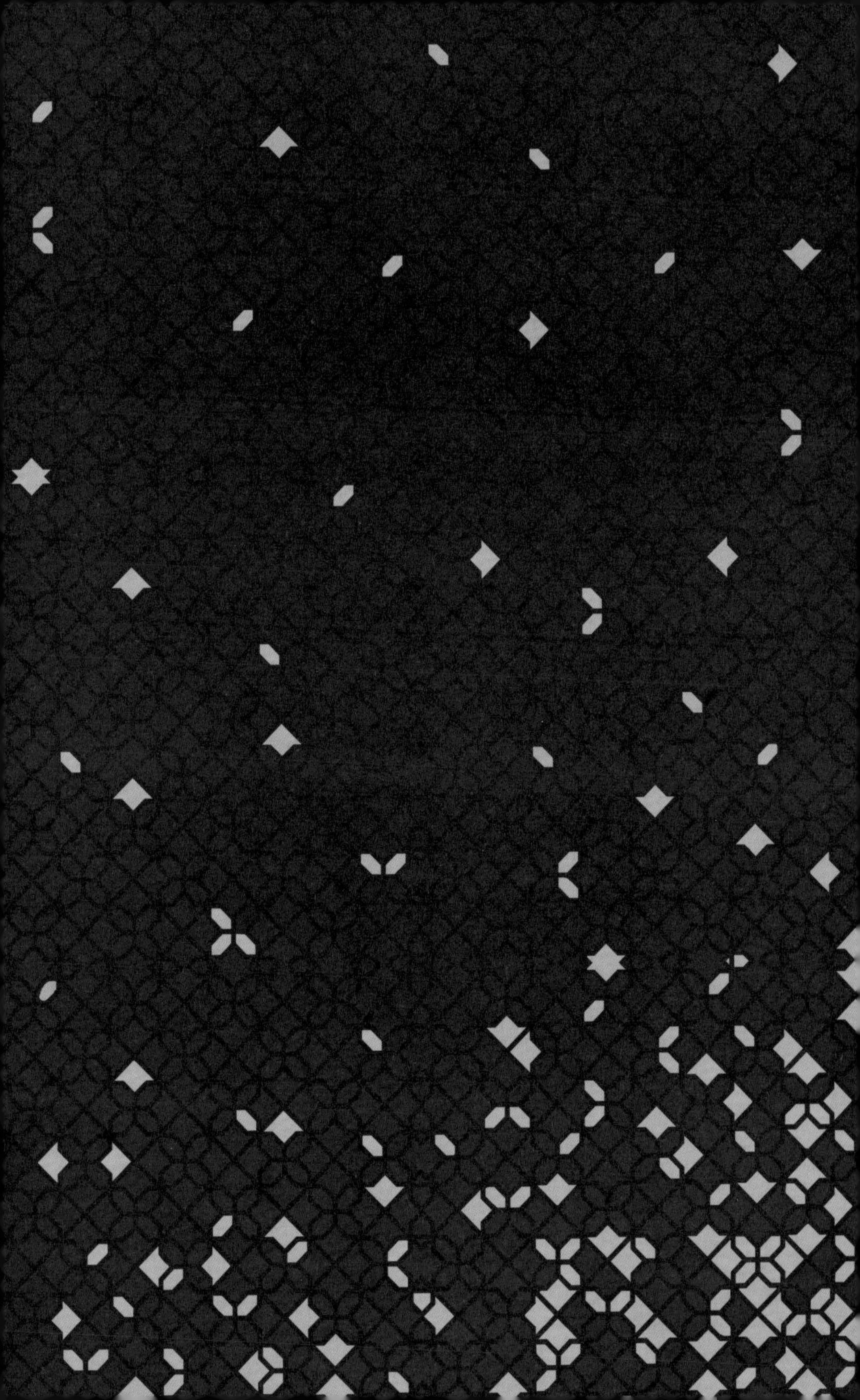

CHAPTER

TWO

SIX MONTHS AGO...
UNLESS ONE OF THE WOODEN DUMMIES HERE INSULTED YOUR HONOR, ELENA...

...I'D SAY YOU'VE WORKED ON YOUR SWORDSMANSHIP ENOUGH FOR THE DAY.
OR THE YEAR.
LIKE YOU'VE EVER SETTLED FOR GOOD ENOUGH, AMELIA.
I AM NOT THE ONE WHO IS TO BE APPOINTED A GREAT GENERAL.
SURELY YOU'VE GOT BETTER THINGS TO STUDY?
PER BEAT ME IN A SWORDFIGHT TODAY.

SWORDS AND MISCHIEF ARE THE ONLY THINGS THAT SISTER OF YOURS IS GOOD AT.
SOMETIMES, I WONDER IF THAT SPARROW EVEN WANTS TO BE A LION.
WE'VE DREAMED OF NOTHING ELSE SINCE WE WERE SMALL.
WE'RE MORE ALIKE THAN YOU THINK, AMELIA.
THAT'S PART OF THE PROBLEM.
SHE WANTS TO BE A LION. SHE JUST DOESN'T WANT TO BE *ME*.

NOW
WHEN I TOLD YOU TO BE FORCEFUL WITH THE COUNCIL, "ELENA"...
...TRYING TO BEHEAD ONE OF THEM WASN'T WHAT I MEANT.
AMELIA!
LISTEN TO ME, THAT GENERAL, FERRIS--
--IS HEADED THIS WAY IN A FEW MINUTES. THE GENERALS WANT TO TALK TO YOU BEFORE RELEASING YOU.
I'M FREE?
NOT EXACTLY.
I TOLD THEM THAT YOU WERE...
TRAUMATIZED BY THE ATTACK AT ESTERPIKE, AND THEY'VE DECIDED "TO CONFINE YOU TO YOUR QUARTERS INSTEAD, UNTIL THE ELECTIONS."
THE GOOD NEWS IS, THE VOTE IS TOMORROW. CAST YOUR BALLOT, AND YOU'RE FREE TO GO.
A BALLOT? I'M RUNNING A BLADE THROUGH FE--

FERRIS WAS HERE WHILE ESTERPIKE WAS BEING ATTACKED. AND BESIDES, HE--
I KNOW WHAT I SAW!
CONTROL YOUR--
NO! I DID WHAT YOU ASKED, BUT I'M DONE!
I SHOULD BE BACK AT ESTERPIKE!
I'M NOT MY SISTER--
NO, BECAUSE ELENA IS DEAD.

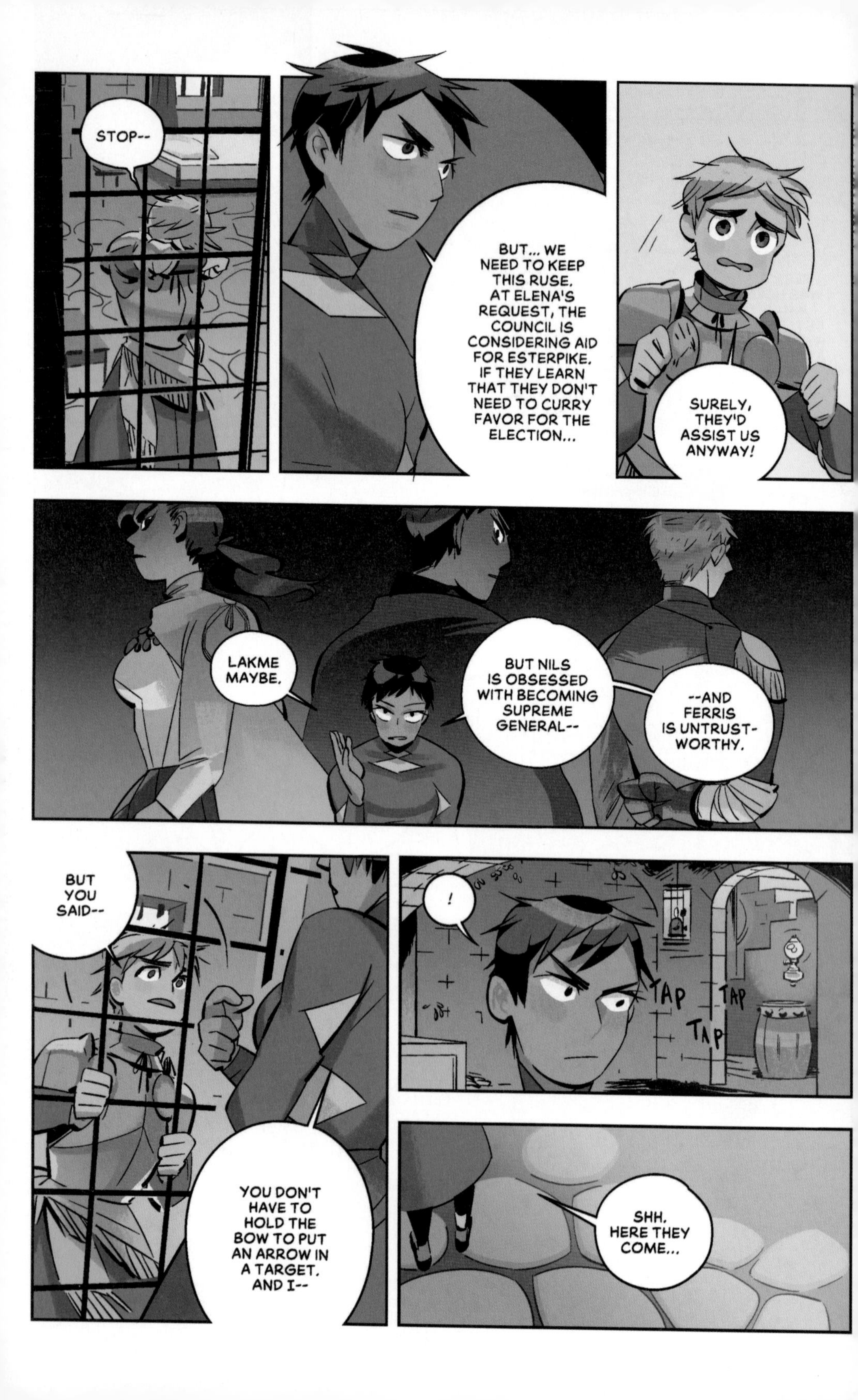
STOP--
BUT... WE NEED TO KEEP THIS RUSE. AT ELENA'S REQUEST, THE COUNCIL IS CONSIDERING AID FOR ESTERPIKE. IF THEY LEARN THAT THEY DON'T NEED TO CURRY FAVOR FOR THE ELECTION...
SURELY, THEY'D ASSIST US ANYWAY!
LAKME MAYBE.
BUT NILS IS OBSESSED WITH BECOMING SUPREME GENERAL--
--AND FERRIS IS UNTRUST-WORTHY.
BUT YOU SAID--
YOU DON'T HAVE TO HOLD THE BOW TO PUT AN ARROW IN A TARGET. AND I--
!
TAP
TAP
TAP
SHH. HERE THEY COME...

DON'T WORRY, FERRIS, MAYBE YOUR BIRD WILL PROTECT YOU.
THAT'S RIGHT, LAKME, MAKE FUN OF THE DISABLED MAN. SIR FLUFF BRINGS ME PEACE.
AS YOU SEE, MY ARM MAKES FOR A FINE PERCH, BUT LITTLE ELSE. IF YOUR COMMANDER STILL SEEKS SATISFACTION--
DIS-ABLED?
I... MUST... RESPECT-FULLY... ER...
ON THE HONOR OF THE LIONS AND MY SISTER...

...I APOLOGIZE, GENERAL FERRIS.
AH... WELL...
THINK NOTHING OF IT, MILADY.
HA! FERRIS, TONGUE-TIED?
I WILL ACCEPT ANY PUNISHMENT...
DON'T RAISE YOUR HEAD JUST YET, ELENA.
YOU'LL HAVE TO MAKE DO WITH A PROMOTION. RISE, GREAT GENERAL.

WHAT IS...?
YOUR SYMBOL OF OFFICE. A FRAGMENT OF THE KEY OF SEASONS.
YOU UNDERSTAND ITS SIGNIFICANCE, OF COURSE?
ELENA'S EDUCATION WAS OF A MORE PRACTICAL SORT, GENERAL NILS.
THAT WILL NOT DO.
GREAT, HERE IT COMES...
WHEN THE WISE EMPRESS DISSOLVED THE MARIAE EMPIRE INTO FOUR SEPARATE NATIONS MAKING UP UNITY...

"...SHE KNEW THAT THEY COULD NOT FORM AN ALLIANCE OF EQUALS IF MARIAE RETAINED ACCESS TO ITS VAULT OF SEASONS.
"THE VAULT HELD THE EMPIRE'S MOST PRIZED TREASURES AND MOST DANGEROUS SECRETS AND WEAPONS.
"SO THE EMPRESS SPLIT THE KEY TO THE VAULT AND DISTRIBUTED A FRAGMENT TO THE GREAT GENERALS OF EACH NATION.
"WHEN UNITY NEEDS A SUPREME GENERAL, THE GREAT GENERALS CHOOSE FROM AMONGST THEMSELVES, AND THE FRAGMENTS ARE USED TO CAST THEIR VOTES.
"THE WINNER RETAINS ALL THE FRAGMENTS, AND SHALL ALONE HAVE ACCESS TO THE SECRETS AND MIGHT OF THE VAULT."

WITH RESPECT, WHAT ESTERPIKE NEEDS IS IMMEDIATE AID, **NOT** MUSTY SECRETS.
WHICH IS WHY I ALREADY CAST MY VOTE,
AND WILL LEAD A FORCE TO ESTERPIKE WITHIN THIS VERY DAY.
TH-THANK YOU! THEN I, TOO, WILL VOTE AND--
ABSOLUTELY NOT.
FERRIS' ABSOLUTION IS WELL AND GOOD, BUT YOU MUST STILL FACE SOME REPRISAL.
THERE WILL BE PLENTY TO OCCUPY YOU IN YOUR QUARTERS-- DOCUMENTS TO SIGN, STATEMENTS TO READ...
YOU CANNOT BE SERIOUS.
WHEN IT COMES TO PAPERWORK, NILS NEVER JOKES.
I'LL GO IN MY COMMANDER'S STEAD, IF YOU'LL HAVE ME, GENERAL.
OF COURSE, AMELIA. IT'LL BE JUST LIKE OLD TIMES.

IT'S DECIDED THEN. WE'LL HAVE AN ESCORT SENT FOR YOU, ELENA, TO BRING YOU TO YOUR ROOM.
AMELIA...
THIS WORKS IN OUR FAVOR. FIND OUT WHAT YOU CAN ABOUT NILS AND FERRIS.
HOW? THEY ORDERED ME CONFINED TO MY ROOM!
AND YOU, OF COURSE, ALWAYS DO AS YOU'RE TOLD.
HEH!
I FEARED YOU WOULDN'T JOIN US IN TIME, CAPTAIN AMELIA.

WHEN HAVE I EVER LET YOU DOWN, GENERAL?
JUST THE ONCE...
...WHEN YOU LEFT ETHREN AND MY SERVICE.
WE BOTH KNOW I WASN'T FIT FOR A COMMAND, LAKME.
NOT WHEN YOU WERE MY AIDE-DE-CAMP.
BUT YOU'VE CHANGED A LOT SINCE THEN.
THE AMELIA I KNEW WOULD HAVE ABANDONED ELENA AFTER HER MISTAKE.

DID YOU THINK ME SO DISLOYAL?
NOT DISLOYAL.
BUT YOU NEVER BOWED, SAVE TO YOUR BETTERS. AND YOU FELT HARDLY ANYONE WAS YOUR BETTER.
IN THAT CASE... I GUESS I HAVE CHANGED.

FIVE YEARS AGO
THE TARID PASS
YOU WON'T BEAT ME THIS TIME, ESTERPIKE.
THIS TIME, I WON'T HAVE A TEAM HOLDING ME BACK.
ISN'T THE POINT OF THIS CAMP TO MAKE US BETTER LEADERS, AMELIA?

THE POINT IS TO FIND THE BEST OF THE BEST.
I'LL MAKE GENERAL LAKME PROUD.
IF SHE SENT YOU HERE, DOESN'T THAT MEAN SHE THINKS HIGHLY OF YOU?
SILENCE!

OW!
BOWS!
IF GENERAL MARTA COMMENDS ME...
...LAKME WILL KNOW I'M READY FOR MY OWN COMMAND.
SO HOW WILL LAKME REACT WHEN MARTA TELLS HER...

...THAT YOUR TEAM HAS WALKED OUT ON YOU TWICE THIS WEEK?
TARGETS!
Tch
YOU...
SPRINT!
SEVEN SORROWS, YOU'RE AS PRICKLY AS A CORAL.
WELL, EXCUSE ME FOR NOT BEING AS POPULAR AS YOU.

huff
huff
WHAT I AM... IS BETTER.
AND ONCE GENERAL MARTA RETURNS FROM HER TRIP TO THE VALLEY I...
huff
huff
HEY! WHAT'S WRO--

GENERAL MARTA!
WE NEED TO GET BACK.
BUT WHAT WILL WE DO?
WE STRIKE.
I REMEMBER THE REPORTS. VERY RECKLESS, SOME SAID.
YOU CAN'T ARGUE WITH THE RESULTS.
NOT I! YOU NEED TO BE BRAZEN TO BE A LEADER.
YES, WELL...

"... THAT'S A FAMILY TRAIT."
SIGH
knock knock!
OK, ON SECOND THOUGHT...
...SEND ME BACK TO THE DUN--
BY THE WISDOM, IT'S REALLY YOU!
OH, MY APOLOGIES MILADY.
I MEAN, GENERAL...
I'VE JUST BEEN SO LOOKING FORWARD TO MEETING YOU!

UH...
WE'VE ALL BEEN BREATHLESS WAITING FOR YOUR ARRIVAL, GENERAL ELENA!
OH, I CAN'T EVEN TELL YOU, SUCH AN INSPIRATION TO US ALL--
OH, UM, THA--
--SOCKED HER MAN RIGHT ON THE NOSE, SHOUTING THE LIONS BATTLE CRY, AND--
BUT THAT'S--
--SO SHE AND I HAD TO DRAW LOTS TO DECIDE WHO TOOK UP YOUR DINNER AND--
--SO MANY QUESTIONS, ABOUT YOUR BATTLES AND--
--YOUR ARMOR, AND DO YOU SLEEP IN IT?
EXCUSE ME, MISS...?

NIKEL, GENERAL. I'M SORRY IF I'M BABBLING I JUST--
NIKEL, I COULD USE YOUR HELP WITH SOMETHING.
WELL, GENERAL FERRIS LEFT STRICT INSTRUC-TIONS THAT--
IT WILL MEAN YOU NEED TO WEAR MY ARMOR FOR A WHILE, THOUGH...

I HOPE GENERAL FERRIS WINS TONIGHT.
YOU JUST WANT TO SEE HIS PRETTY FACE HERE MORE OFTEN.
AND, SILLY, SINCE FERRIS DOESN'T WANT TO WIN.
RIGHT? HE'S BACKED NILS FOR SUPREME GENERAL FROM THE START.
DO YA EVEN SEE ALL THESE CAMBRIAN LAMPS?
SAW ONE A' THESE FETCHING TWO GOLD AT A FAIR.
GOLD!
GENERAL FERRIS ORDERED THEM SPECIAL...
AND IF HE'S ALREADY DECORATING THIS PLACE, HE MUST THINK HE'S GOT THE ELECTION IN THE BAG!
GOT YOU!

BEEN WATCHING YOU SNOOP AROUND, GIRL. I'VE NEVER SEEN YOU BEFORE. SO I'M THINKING THERE'S ONLY ONE THING YOU COULD BE...
YOU'RE ONE OF THE HEAD MAID'S NEW SPIES, AREN'TCHA?
RATS, YOU FOUND ME OUT.
I KNEW IT!
WELL YOU TELL YOUR BOSS THAT THE WINTER CHAMBER IS ALL SET FOR THE POST-ELECTION BALL!
IT'S FUNNY THOUGH... I SHOULD HAVE HEARD OF ANY NEW MAID HIRES...
OH! I... I DON'T THINK YOU'RE READY FOR THE BALL AT ALL.

WHATCHA MEAN BY THAT, HUH?
I HEARD GENERAL FERRIS WANTED THE BALL MOVED...
...TO THE, UH, OTHER CHAMBER.
WHAT?!
AND WHEN EXACTLY WAS YOUR BOSS GOING TO TELL ME THAT, HUH?
SHE WASN'T.
WHAT?
THINK ABOUT IT.
WANTS ME TO TAKE THE FALL, HUH? I'LL SHOW OLD MARY.
PACK IT ALL UP! MOVE EVERYTHING TO THE SUMMER CHAMBER!
DOUBLE TIME!
groan
augh
THERE YOU GO. NOW IF ONLY I COULD FIGURE OUT...

"...WHERE NIKEL RAN OFF TO..."
BARBARIANS! LAY DOWN YOUR WEAPONS! OR YOU WILL FEEL THE ARMORED MIGHT OF THE GREAT GENERAL NIK--
knock knock
--EEE...!
GENERAL ELENA? MAY I HAVE A WORD?
VAULT TAKE ME, THAT'S GENERAL FERRIS' VOICE!
WHATDOI DOWHATDOIDO WHATDOI-!
YOU'RE, UH, DRESSED. WILL YOU JOIN ME FOR A WALK?
I'M SURE YOU'VE SPENT ENOUGH TIME IN THAT ROOM TO LAST A LIFETIME.
I'LL TAKE YOUR SILENCE AS A YES THEN?
GOOD. I'D LIKE TO CLEAR THE AIR BETWEEN US. MAYBE IF YOU KNEW A BIT ABOUT ME...

FIFTEEN MINUTES AND THREE FLOORS OF THE CASTLE LATER...
...SO THAT'S THE STORY OF HOW I CAME TO JOIN THE ARMY, EVEN WITH THIS BAD ARM.
OF COURSE, HOW I BECAME A GENERAL IS ANOTHER STORY ENTIRELY...
BUT I HAVE A FEELING I MAY BE BORING YOU. THAT IS NOT MY INTENT, BELIEVE ME.
ELENA, WE'RE NOT SO DIFFERENT.
I TOO VALUE FAMILY ABOVE ALL.
I'VE CONVINCED NILS TO ALLOW YOU TO CAST YOUR VOTE EARLY.
THE ANTECHAMBER OF SEASONS.

I KNOW BETTER THAN TO TRY TO SWAY YOU, ELENA.
SO JUST SET YOUR FRAGMENT INTO ONE OF THE PODIUMS, AND YOU CAN HEAD BACK TO ESTERPIKE.
LAKME'S ALREADY VOTED AND PLACED HER FRAGMENT.
I'VE ALREADY HAD A HORSE READIED FOR...
WHY ARE YOU BACKING AWAY? ELENA, WE NEED A NEW SUPREME GENERAL. IF THE FORCE THAT ATTACKED ESTERPIKE WAS BUT THE VANGUARD--
GET BACK HERE!

WOMAN, YOU'VE DEFIED ME--
--FOR THE LAST TIME!
WOULD THAT I COULD...
I'D DEAL WITH YOU WITH MORE ELEGANCE.
BUT OUR PLANS ARE AT A DELICATE STAGE
YOU ARE TOO UNPRE-DICTABLE, ELENA
LUCKILY, YOU'VE ALREADY ATTACKED ME ONCE...

...SIMPLE ENOUGH TO SAY I KILLED YOU IN SELF DEFEN--
NO, WAIT!

THIS IS A MISTAKE!

WHO THE BLAZES ARE YOU?!

SHE'S THE LAST PERSON YOU'LL EVER HURT.

I DON'T KNOW WHAT'S GOING ON, BUT...
YOU ONLY NEED TO KNOW ONE THING, SCUMLORD!
YOU'LL PAY FOR WHAT YOU DID TO ELENA!
TO ELE--?
AH.
NOW IT ALL MAKES SENSE.
YOU'RE NOT ELENA.
YOU'RE THE SISTER, THE SPARROW...
THE FAILURE.

HYAH
AAH
EVEN IF I CAN'T TAKE YOU DOWN...
...ESTERPIKE WILL BE READY FOR YOU NEXT TIME.
YOU TRULY ARE AN IDIOT.
YOU STILL THINK THAT I'M THE ONE THAT ATTACKED YOUR PRECIOUS VILLAGE.
I KNOW WHAT I SAW!
AND HOW MANY PEOPLE TODAY PASSED YOU AND "SAW" A MAID?
YOU'RE NOT THE ONLY ONE CAPABLE OF DECEPTION, PER OF ESTERPIKE...

"YOU'RE NOT THE ONLY ONE CAPABLE OF SURPRISE."
JUST A LITTLE FURTHER. WE SHOULD SEE THE VILLAGE RIGHT OVER THIS--
THIS...
...THIS CAN'T BE...

OVER THERE!
"YOU'RE NOT THE ONLY ONE WITH FAMILY THAT WOULD DIE FOR YOU."
AS I WAS TELLING YOUR STAND-IN HERE...
THE TWO OF US ARE MORE ALIKE THAN YOU'D THINK.

I THINK I HAVE MORE IN COMMON WITH YOUR BROTHER. AFTER ALL...
...HE'S ABOUT TO BE DOWN A SIBLING.

CHAPTER THREE

CLANG
CLANG

CLANG

CLANG
CLK
CLANG

CAN'T BEAT A ONE ARMED MAN?
CLANG
WHAT WOULD DEAR, DEAD ELENA SAY?

YEAH? WELL, I COULD BEAT MY SISTER.
EVEN IF YOU HAD TEN ARMS--
--YOU'D BE HALF THE WARRIOR SHE WAS!
SO I THINK SHE'D SAY: KICK HIS--
WHOA!
NO NEED TO GUESS.
KICK

YOU CAN ASK HER YOURSELF.
PUSH
NO!
SLASH

NIKEL!

ONE MORE...

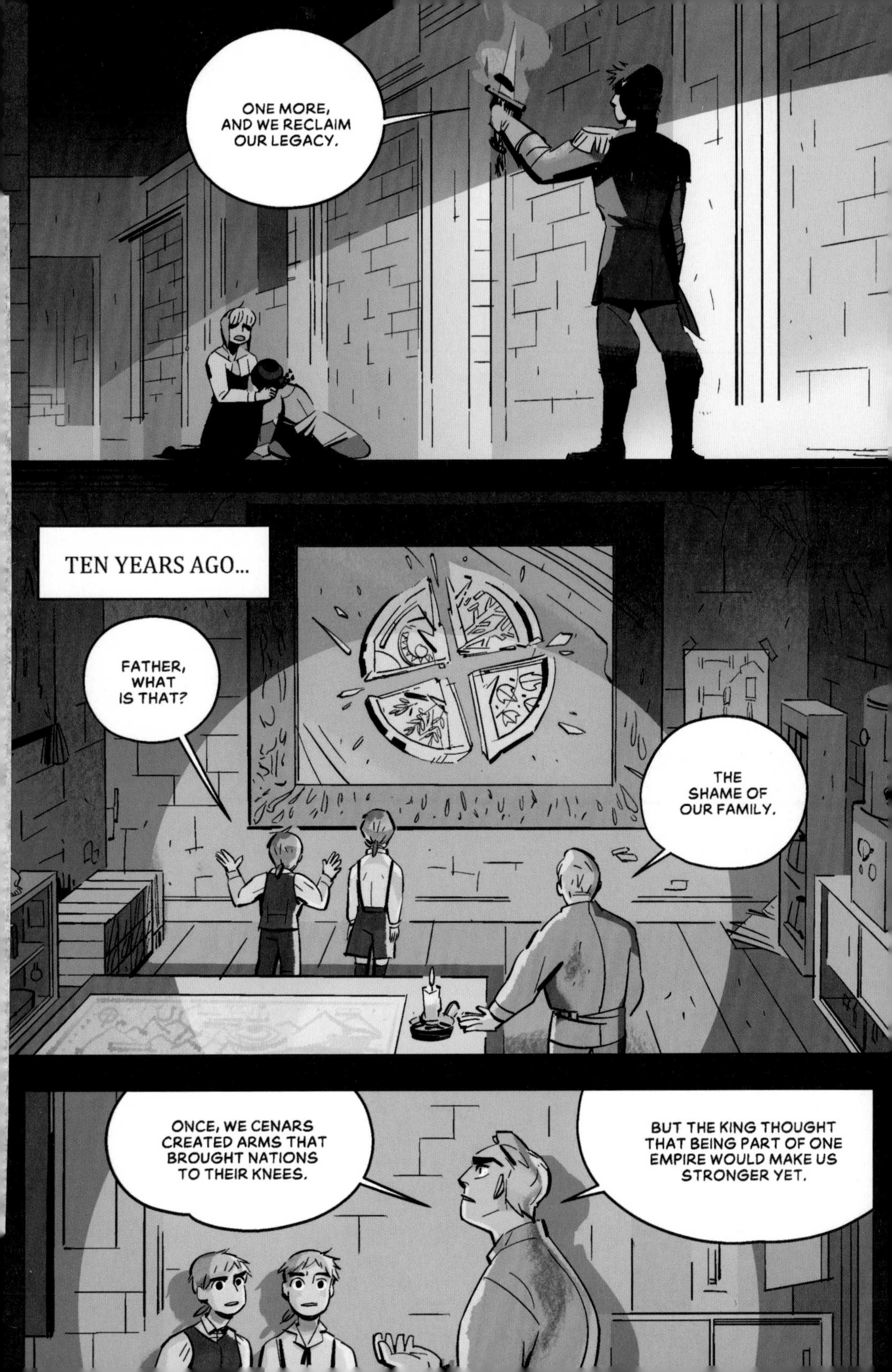
ONE MORE, AND WE RECLAIM OUR LEGACY.
TEN YEARS AGO...
FATHER, WHAT IS THAT?
THE SHAME OF OUR FAMILY.
ONCE, WE CENARS CREATED ARMS THAT BROUGHT NATIONS TO THEIR KNEES.
BUT THE KING THOUGHT THAT BEING PART OF ONE EMPIRE WOULD MAKE US STRONGER YET.

BUT THEIR OH-SO WISE EMPRESS TURNED THE EMPIRE INTO A SQUABBLING ALLIANCE.
AND NOW OUR GREAT WORKS LANGUISH IN THE VAULT OF AN EMPIRE THAT NO LONGER EXISTS.
SO WHAT SHOULD WE DO, FATHER?
GROW. SMART AND STRONG. SO THAT WHEN IT IS TIME TO ACT...
FIVE YEARS AGO...
...YOU ARE READY.
SO LET US COME WITH YOU!

DAD!
NO. WE PINNED OUR HOPES ON A SINGLE PLAN BEFORE, AND THAT WAS A MISTAKE. EACH OF US HAS A PART TO PLAY.
AND IF YOU AND YOUR ASH WARRIORS FAIL, FATHER?
THEN...
...OUR BLOOD WILL PAVE YOUR PATH...
...TO VICTORY.

NIKEL! NIKEL, WAKE... UP!
NGH... LIONS...
TAP
TAP
TAP
TAP
TAP

FERRIS MAY HAVE WHAT HE WANTS,
BUT HE'S STILL GOING TO COME AFTER YOU--

--BOTH OF YOU, TO BE PRECISE.
TAP
TAP

KILLING ME IS ONE THING. HOW'RE YOU GOING TO EXPLAIN NIKEL?

SHE'S OBVIOUSLY A CONSPIRATOR.
SHE'S EVEN WEARING YOUR ARMOR!
YOU CAN'T OUTFIGHT ME. YOU CAN'T OUTWIT ME.
P-POOP HEAD!
SERIOUSLY?
I EVEN HAD THIS WING OF THE CASTLE CLEARED. JUST IN CASE.
I'VE PREPARED FOR EVERYTHING! EXCEPT FOR HOW GOOD IT WILL FEEL--

--WHEN I FINALLY--

--KILL YOU!

WHY--
WHY ARE
YOU ALL...
THE FEAST
IS IN THE
WINTER--
GENERAL FERRIS
ATTACKED A MAID!
HE'S GONE MAD!
WAIT! THIS ISN'T
WHAT IT LOOKS LIKE!
SHE'S NOT A MAID,
SHE'S--

--GONE.

PER OF
ESTERPIKE...!
SIR
FERRIS!

... IT IS OF NO CONSEQUENCE.
ARE YOU ALL RIGHT?
BUT THE PLAN--
THE PLAN MOVES FORWARD, BUT AT A QUICKER PACE. WHILE I GATHER THE FRAGMENTS...
...YOU TRIGGER THE LAMPS.
"THE TIME FOR SUBTERFUGE IS OVER."
clk
clk
click

I'M SORRY! IF YOU HADN'T LET ME WEAR YOUR ARMOR--
STOP THAT.
I'M THE ONE AT FAULT HERE. AS. ALWAYS.
I PUT YOU IN DANGER WITH ANOTHER ONE OF MY HARE-BRAINED SCHEMES, JUST LIKE I DID MY SISTER, AND NOW...
...SHE'S DEAD AND I'M... I'M...
DAMNIT!
WHAT THE HELL CAN I EVEN DO ON MY...

WE'LL MAKE IT THROUGH.

OF COURSE! IF MILADY ELENA SAYS--
WAIT. WHAT'S THAT SOUND...
CLICK
CLICK
CLICK

click
click
BOOOOMMMMM

ESTERPIKE
IT'S GONE.
I'M SORRY, AMELIA.
GONE DOESN'T MEAN DEAD. ESTERPIKE WAS ORIGINALLY A CARAVAN.
THEY COULD HAVE... MIGHT HAVE...
THIS WAS A CENAR DESTROYER. THOSE BOMBS HAVEN'T BEEN SEEN SINCE THE TRUCE OF ICE.
BUT I'VE SEEN THE OLD REPORTS... DEATH WOULD HAVE BEEN INSTANTANEOUS.
IS THAT MEANT TO CONSOLE ME?
IT'S MEANT TO KEEP YOU FROM FALSE HOPE.
GENERAL!
WE BELIEVE WE'VE FOUND THE SPOOR OF THESE VILLAINS. THEY ARE NOT FAR.

ALL FORCES, MOUNT UP. WE MUST KEEP ANY CENAR WEAPONS FROM THE GATES OF UNITY.
YOU MUST. MY DUTY IS TO THE SURVIVORS.
I ALREADY TOLD YOU--
MY DUTY. IS TO. THE SURVIVORS.
IT'S WHAT SHE WOULD... WANT ME TO DO.
YOU REALLY HAVE CHANGED. VERY WELL.
UNTIL NEXT WE PART WAYS, AMELIA OF ETHERN.

THE TARID PASS

THEY OUTNUMBER US, GENERAL. IT'S TOO RISKY.
THERE'S ALWAYS A WAY TO WIN.
IF WE FAIL, YOU SCOUTS ARE TO HEAD TO UNITY.
WE WILL NOT LEAVE YOU TO--
AM I NOT YOUR GENERAL? SHOULD I ASK YOU TO SLIT MY THROAT, YOUR ONLY CONCERN SHOULD BE THE BLADE TO USE.
CHIN UP, SOLDIER. IF A ROOKIE LION COULD HOLD THE TARID PASS...

"WHAT MAKES YOU THINK WE CAN'T DO THE SAME?"
READY THE ANTI-CAVALRY EQUIPMENT.

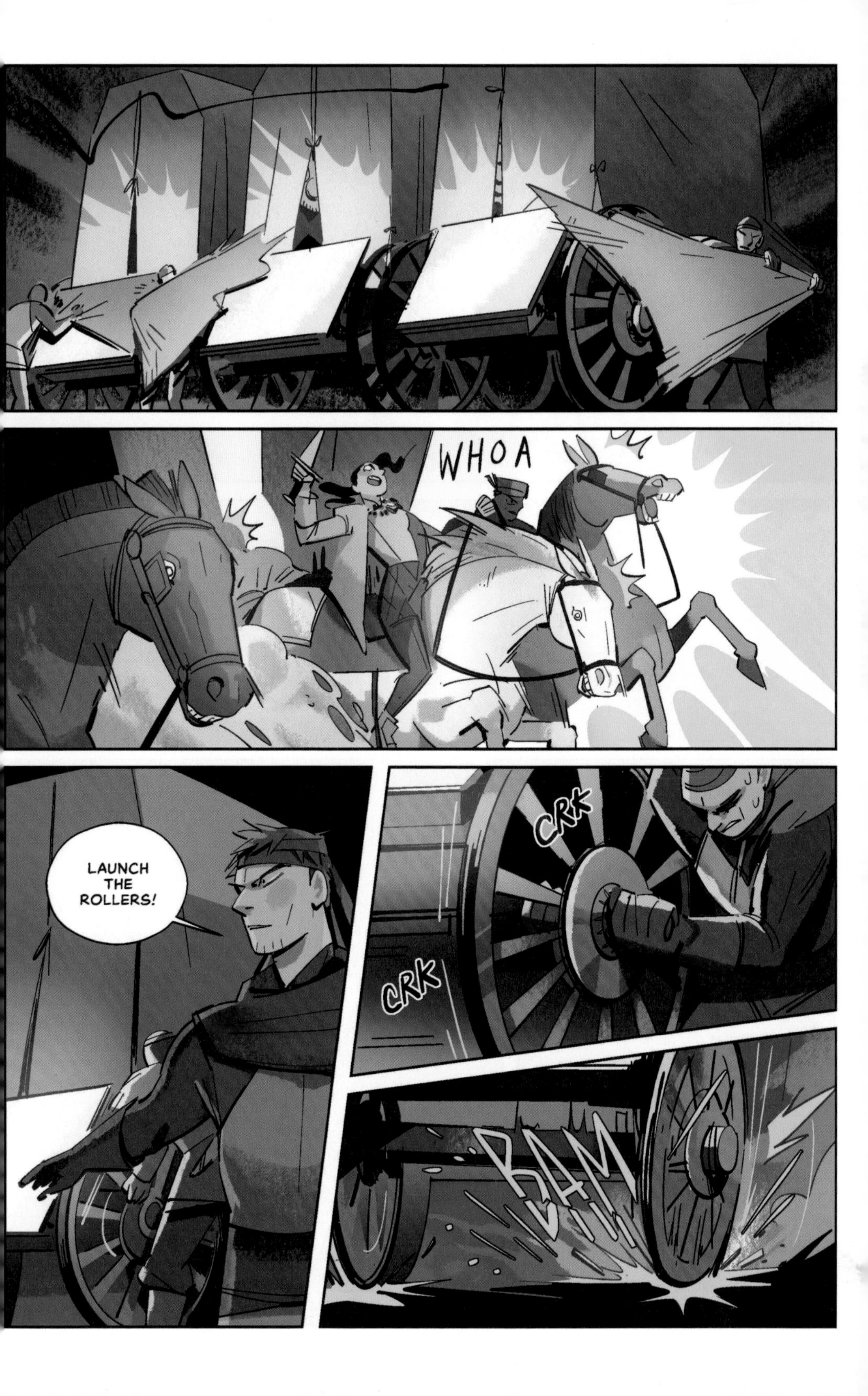
WHOA
LAUNCH THE ROLLERS!
CRK
CRK
BAM

FWOOMM
CRASH
FSSSS
UGH
CLINK
DISMOUNT! FORM ON ME!

CLINK
FSSSSH
CLANG
COUGH FORM ON ME!
CLANG
CL
CLANG
CLANG
CLANG
CLANG

F-FERRIS?
NO, YOU'RE...
I GET IT NOW.
YOU'VE ALREADY LOST!
YOU'VE SHOWN YOUR
HAND COMPLETELY, ALL
YOUR LITTLE TRICKS...
UNITY WILL
BE READY!
SPLASH
WHAT?!

AUGH!
THIS IS WHY YOUR PEOPLE ARE WEAK, GENERAL.
YOU THINK WEAPONS SHOULD BE HIDDEN.
YEAAA RGH!
WEAPONS ARE TO BE USED! TO MAIM, TO KILL--
--TO SEND A MESSAGE.
AUHHH

G-GENERAL...
WE'RE COMING.
TWO YEARS AGO...
TOOK YOUR TIME, BROTHER.
IT'S NOT EASY LEADING AN ARMY TO AN AMBUSH, FAHRIS.
IS THAT OUR NOTORIOUS BANDIT LEADER?

AS PROMISED. WITH THIS ACHIEVEMENT, AND THE DEATH OF SO MANY SENIOR KNIGHTS, YOUR PATH TO PROMOTION IS SET.
THUMP
Roll
Roll
AND WIPING OUT A CAMBRIAN ARMY IS SURE TO BRING MANY ROGUES FLOCKING TO YOUR BANNER.
I'D RATHER THE COMPANY OF BRIGANDS THAN THE POLITICIANS YOU HAVE TO CHARM.
EVERY SACRIFICE IS A SHOW OF OUR RESOLVE. NOW, QUIT STALLING.
MUST I?
AN ARM IS A SMALL PRICE TO PAY TO ALLAY ANY SUSPICIONS.
FOR CAMBRIA, BROTHER.
FOR CAMBRIA.

ROUND UP EVERY CAMBRIAN SOLDIER AND STAFF MEMBER. WE MUST KNOW FOR SURE IF--
NILS, NILS, NILS...
TALKING WHEN YOU SHOULD BE ACTING, ONCE AGAIN.
IT'S A BAD HABIT.
IT'S WHY YOU'D HAVE MADE A HORRIBLE SUPREME GENERAL.
SHOULD I TAKE THIS AS AN OFFICIAL WITHDRAWAL OF SUPPORT?
GO. RALLY WITH THE OTHERS.
ALL I WANTED WAS FOR THE KEY TO BE WHOLE AGAIN. YOU CAN HAVE YOUR PAPER RANK...
THE WEAPON PLANS OF OUR FOREFATHERS ARE WHERE POWER REALLY LIES.
THOSE PLANS WERE LOCKED AWAY FOR A REASON, FERRIS. THEY ARE TOO--

YOU DARE
LECTURE ME
ON HISTORY?
CAMBRIA HAS BEEN
ITS PRIME MOVER FOR
A CENTURY!
CRUNCH
BUT YOU
LESSER NATIONS
ARE BUCKING
MULES!
ONLY INTERESTED
IN PASTURES YOU'VE
ALREADY GRAZED
TO DIRT.
SO YOU WILL
BE TREATED LIKE
ANIMALS, THEN,
WITH A FIRM--
BAM
WHA?

--HAAAAAAAGH!
MISS ME?
BECAUSE I SURE DIDN'T--
OOOF!
RRRRARGH!
AGH

RIGHT. NO MORE TALKING.
ARG
BAM
!

!
ELENA!
ALLOW ME
TO ASSIST--

THROW YOUR FRAGMENT OFF THE BALCONY!
WHAT? BUT THIS IS A PRICELESS HISTORICAL--
NILS! THROW IT!
WBL
WBL
WBL
HAH! I GOT IT, I--

I...
WHEN YOU SEE MY SISTER...
ASK HER IF SHE'S PROUD OF ME.
M...
...MY BROTHER...
...IS COMING.

IS HE NOW?
GOOD.

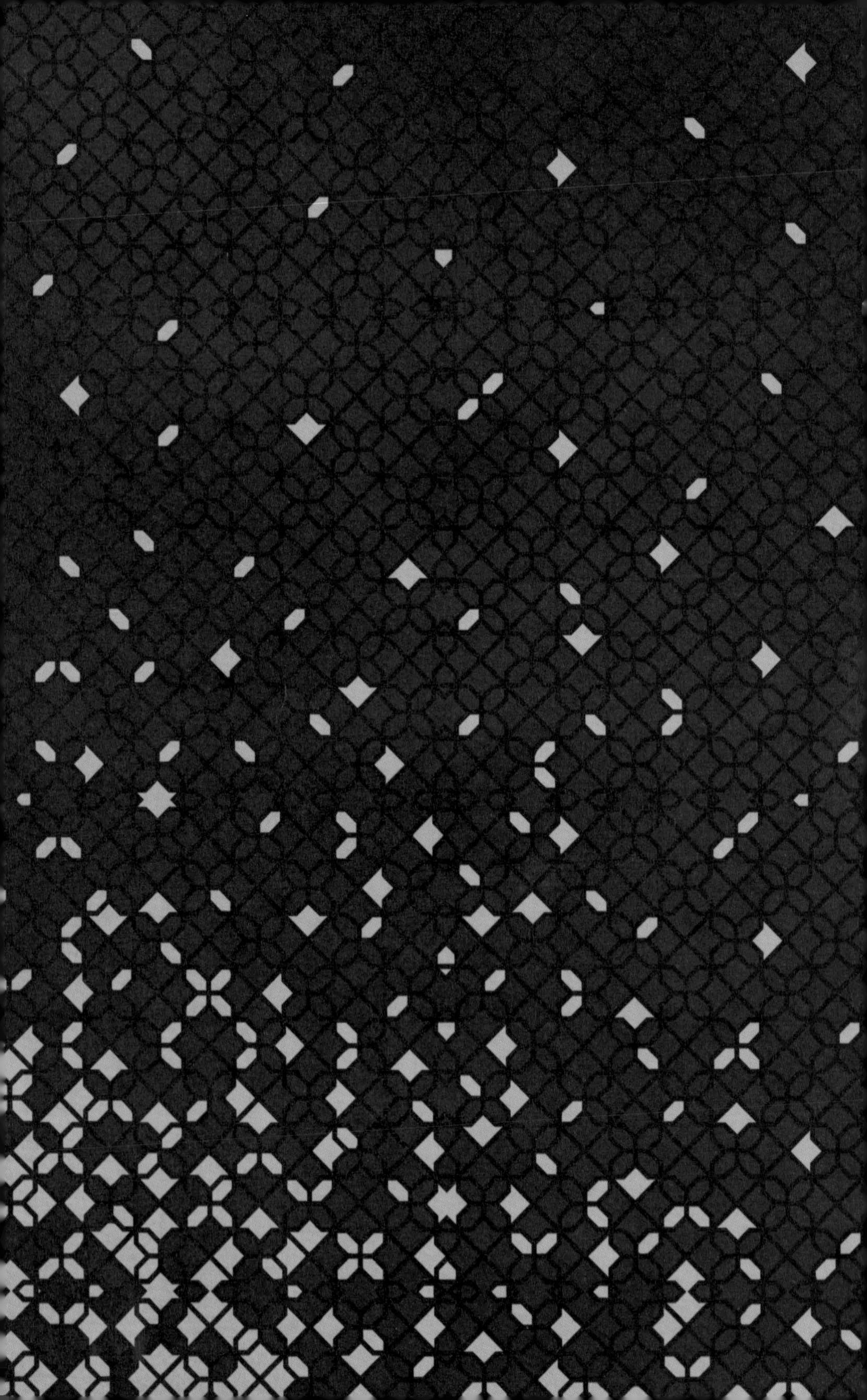

CHAPTER

FOUR

THE DAY IS BRIGHT AND FULL OF PROMISE.
I KNOW IT IS A LIE.
...COMPLETED THE DETENTION OF KNOWN CAMBRIANS IN THE RANKS...
...BUT MANY CLAIM LOYALTY TO UNITY.
WHAT DID YOU EXPECT THOSE TRAITORS TO SAY?
IF THE ASH WARRIORS ARE COMING, CAN WE AFFORD TO JAIL A FOURTH OF OUR SOLDIERS?
STILL NO WORD FROM LAKME?
NONE, GENERAL NILS. AND WE STILL HAVEN'T FOUND GENERAL ELENA...
CONFOUND THAT GIRL...

"... WHY CAN'T SHE EVER BE WHERE SHE'S SUPPOSED TO BE?"
FOR THE SAFETY OF UNITY,
EVERY CAMBRIAN IN THE RANKS MUST BE DULY DETAINED.
WHAT?
PLEASE UNDERSTAND.
BUT...
WE'RE LOYAL TO UNITY! OUR FAMILY HAS LIVED IN MARIAE FOR--
THIS IS A TEMPORARY MEASURE. WE APPRECIATE THE COOPERATION OF THOSE AMONG YOU WHO ARE INDEED LOYAL.
I--
SIS?
I WANT TO GO HOME!

PLEASE REMAIN CALM!
HE'S JUST SCARED! WE ALL ARE. PLEASE--
LET GO OF ME! SIS!
LAYING A HAND ON A PALACE GUARD PROVES YOUR DISLOYALTY, CAMBRIAN.
NO! THIS IS WRONG! SOMEBODY--
HEY! WHAT'S THE BIG-?
L-LADY ELENA!
YOU WANT TO ROUGH PEOPLE UP? THERE'S AN ARMY ON ITS WAY. DO I NEED TO TEACH YOU WHERE TO POINT YOUR SWORDS?
GENERAL NILS ORDERED US--
YEAH? WELL I'M GENERAL, TOO, AND I SAY FORGET THAT. IF NILS HAS A PROBLEM WITH THAT, WELL...

"...I'LL MAKE SURE HE KNOWS WHERE TO FIND ME."
WE MUST MOVE CAUTIOUSLY. QUESTION THE PRISONERS FURTHER WHILE WE AWAIT THE RETURN OF--
YOU WILL WAIT IN VAIN, GENERAL NILS.
GENERAL LAKME IS DEAD. AND I FEAR WE ARE SOON TO FOLLOW.
THE ASH WARRIORS... HAVE CENAR BOMBS...
...AND THEY ARE RIGHT ON MY HEELS.
GENERAL!
THE ASH WARRIOR ARMY APPROACHES!

AND GENERAL ELENA, SHE...
"SHE WENT TO MEET THEM! ALONE!"

HEY, ASH WANNABES!
I CHALLENGE YOUR LEADER TO A DUEL!
WHO IS THIS CRAZY KNIGHT?
THAT SWORD...
SIR...?
GIVE ME THAT.
I SEE.
MY BROTHER IS DEAD.

"COME ON, PER."
"FOCUS."
SEND YOUR TOADIES BACK, BROTHER OF FERRIS.

"OUR TIME IS NOW, FAHRIS..."
"WE RECLAIM OUR LEGACY."
AND WHY WOULD I DO THAT, SISTER TO ELENA?

BECAUSE I HAVE WHAT YOU WANT...
...AND IF YOU DON'T GIVE ME WHAT I WANT--
WELL, I'M NO WISE EMPRESS. SO WHEN I BREAK THINGS...
CRK--K
THEY DON'T GET PUT BACK TOGETHER.
ALL RIGHT, LITTLE SPARROW.
WE'LL PLAY YOUR GAME. BUT DO YOU SERIOUSLY THINK YOU CAN BEST ME?
FUNNY...

THAT'S WHAT YOUR BROTHER SAID!
YES, HE ALWAYS WAS THE TALKER.
MY TALENTS LIE ELSEWHERE.
BAMM
URGH!
GENERAL, WHAT SHOULD WE DO?
WE WAIT, ONE WAY OR ANOTHER...

"...THIS SHOULDN'T TAKE LONG."
CLK

WHAT ARE YOU EVEN FIGHTING FOR, LITTLE SPARROW? YOUR SISTER IS DEAD.
YOUR TOWN IS DEAD.
WHAT? YOU'RE LY--
I'D TELL YOU TO ASK LAKME... BUT I DEALT WITH YOUR GENERAL AND HER TROOPS AS WELL.
AND THE CENAR FAMILY DOESN'T LEAVE SURVIVORS.

ESTER-
PIKE...
AMELIA...
SHP
YES. ACCEPT IT, LITTLE SPARROW. YOUR FAILURE. AND NOW--YOUR DEA--
NO...
WHAT...?

LIONS--!

--ROAR!
I-I KNEW YOU WEREN'T DEAD! STUPID, TARDY, WONDERFUL AMELIA...
sniffle
HEY! GET BACK HERE!

KEEP HER OFF ME. I MUST REACH THE BOMBS. EVEN IF I DIE HERE...
"...I'LL TAKE THOSE DAMN LIONS WITH ME."
YOU...
...YOU DUEL DITCHER!
GET OFF ME YOU--!
GRR!
WHOOSH
SSHOOOOMM

GO! HE MUST NOT REACH THE BOMBS!

YOU SMUG SON OF A...
!
HA!
YOU MUST BE JOKING.
YOU WEAR ELENA'S ARMOR, NOW YOU THINK YOU'RE HER EQUAL WITH THE BOW?
A WISE WOMAN ONCE TOLD ME: YOU DON'T HAVE TO SHOOT THE BOW...
"...TO PUT AN ARROW IN THE TARGET."

YEEARGH!
TCK
WHO--?
GOT YOU, YOU BASTARD. NOW, PER...
"...ROAR!"

YIELD, CAMBRIAN!
NEVER AGAIN. NO SURRENDER.
NOT FROM ME.

FINE BY ME.

"DID YOU SEE, ELENA?"
"DID I DO OKAY?"
"DID I MAKE UP FOR IT?"
"I MISS YOU."
"I WISH I KNEW WHAT YOU'D SAY..."

THREE MONTHS LATER
SHE'D SAY GET TO WORK.
HA HA HA HA
HA HA HA HA!
BUT--
--ELENA WOULD ALSO SAY HOW PROUD SHE IS OF ALL OF YOU. FOR SURVIVING.
FOR GETTING BACK ON YOUR FEET.
FOR USING THE WHEELS BENEATH YOUR HOMES NOT ONLY TO LEAVE, BUT TO RETURN.

AND I, TOO, PROMISE TO RETURN.
WHILE I RIDE TO UNITY TONIGHT, I SHALL BE BACK IN THREE DAYS--
--AND WE SHALL CELEBRATE OUR NEW BEGINNING AS ELENA WOULD HAVE WANTED US TO.
A FINE SPEECH, GREAT GENERAL.
THANK YOU, GREAT GENERAL.
I'M STILL SURPRISED YOU CAME PERSONALLY.
WELL, I HAD TO BE SURE ESTERPIKE WAS SENDING THE REAL "GENERAL AMELIA."
TOUCHÉ.
I ALSO WANTED TO PERSONALLY DELIVER THE NEWS THAT ETHERN HAS CHOSEN LAKME'S SUCCESSOR.
NIKEL!
IT'S INEVE.
LAKME'S WARD?
AH. I TAKE IT YOU'RE FAMILIAR WITH HOW SHE FEELS ABOUT YOU?

SHE'S NEVER LIKED ME... BUT NOW SHE BLAMES ME FOR LAKME'S DEATH....
...FOR ABANDONING HER.
I LONG FOR THE DAYS WHEN THE PEOPLE I WORKED WITH DIDN'T WANT TO KILL EACH OTHER.
I HAVE NO ISSUE WITH INEVE. AND AS ANGRY AS SHE IS, SHE WON'T BE SNEAKING BOMBS INTO THE CASTLE.
ON THAT NOTE, ANY WORD FROM CAMBRIA?
NOTHING. BUT THEN, I'M NOT THE MOST POPULAR MAN IN CAMBRIA. BUT IF SOMEONE ELSE APPROACHED THEM--
--SOMEONE WHO STOOD AGAINST THE SEQUESTRATION I ORDERED...
ON THAT NOTE, I WAS HOPING TO SPEAK WITH YOUR SECOND.
I'LL LET HER PUNCH ME AGAIN IF SHE'LL BE OUR ENVOY.
SHE'S GOT THE DAY OFF.
IT'S HER BIRTHDAY...

"...AND SHE'S SPENDING IT WITH FAMILY."
!
THWACK
GRRR...
STUPID WIND...
Vita
Vita
EIENA
SHUT UP, SIS.
FFF
AARGH!

YES!
WOOHOO! WHO'S THE BEST ARCHER, HUH?
WHO'S THE BESTIE-BESTEST?
I'M NOT SURE--
--BUT YOU'RE CERTAINLY THE MOST PERSISTENT ONE.

BOO! IT'S MY BIRTHDAY. NO STINGY GENERALS ALLOWED!
STINGY? AND HERE I CAME ALL THIS WAY TO GIVE YOU SOMETHING.
THAT'S... ELENA'S...
BUT WE LEFT THE ARMOR IN UNITY FOR THE MEMORIAL...
I DIDN'T SAY THEY COULD HAVE ALL OF IT.

BUT... BUT I CAN'T... I'M NOT... NOT HER...
NO.
YOU'RE PER OF ESTERPIKE. SISTER OF ELENA.
A SPARROW THAT ROARS AS LOUD AS ANY LION.
NOW, COME ON.
THEY'VE ALREADY STARTED WITHOUT US.

THE END

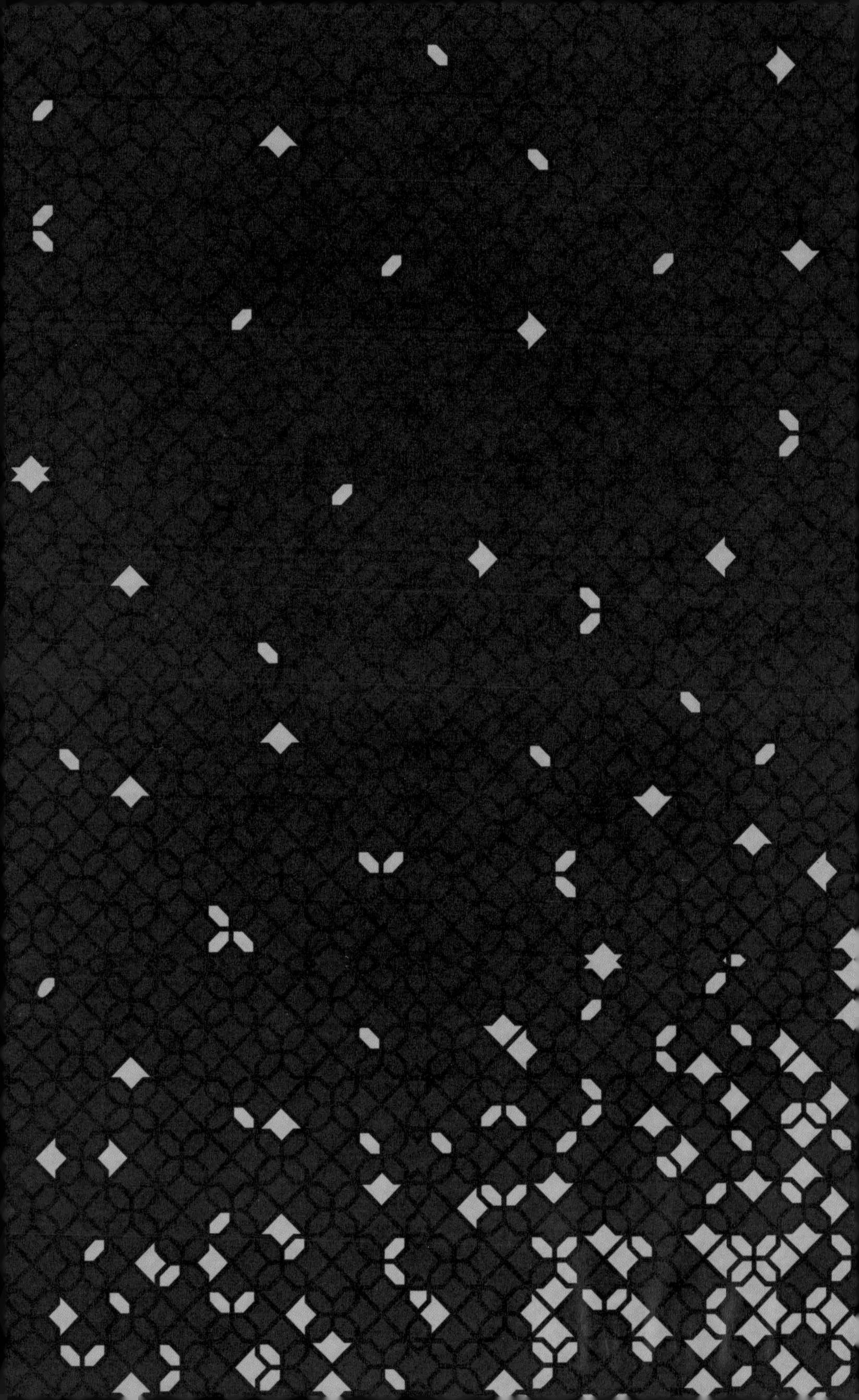

EXTRA STRIPS & EARLY DRAFTS

MIRROR IMAGE
AMELIA!
!
PER, YOU CUT YOUR HAIR...
YEAH! I TOTALLY LOOK MATURE AND COOL, RIGHT?
COOLER THAN MY SISTER, RIGHT?
OH, DID YOU PLAY WITH FIREWORKS AGAIN?
SSSSH!
DIFFERENCES BETWEEN PER AND ELENA
PER
SCRUFFY HEDGEHOG
ELENA
SMOOTH HEDGEHOG

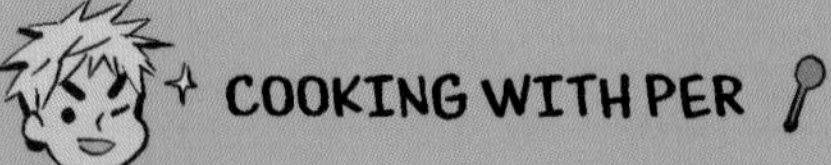
COOKING WITH PER

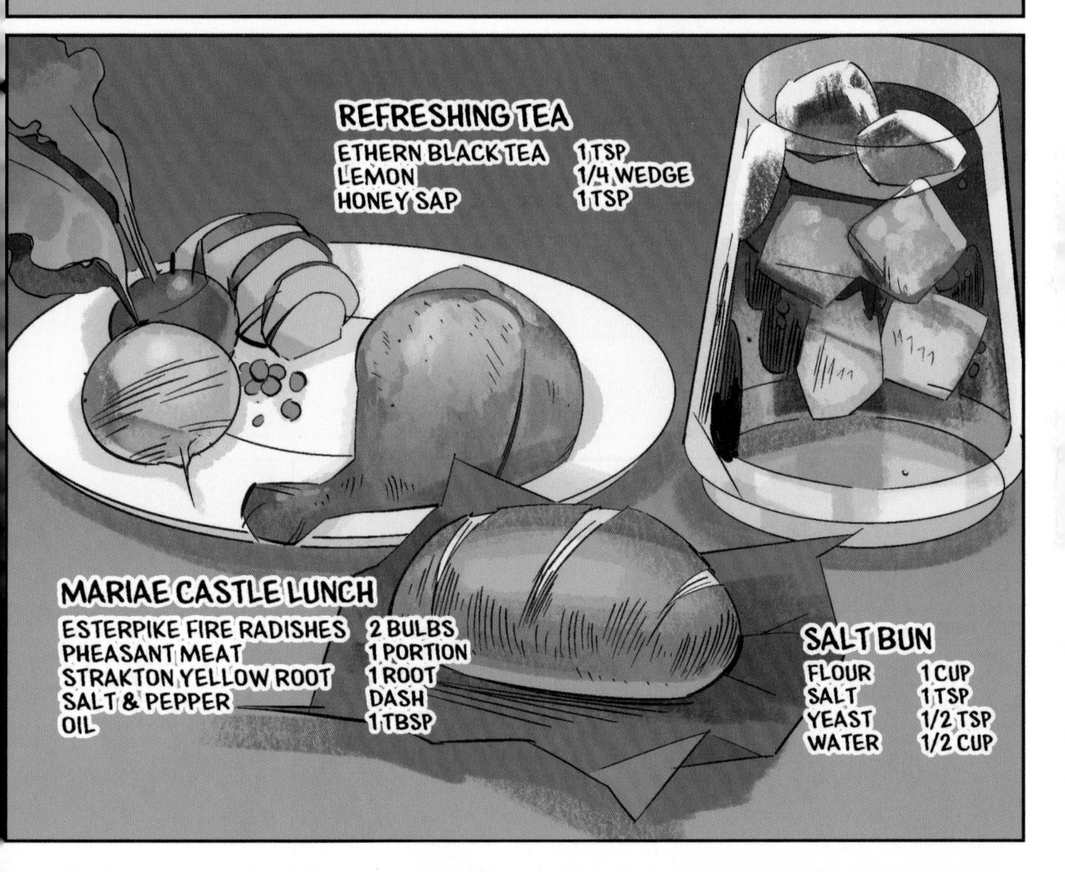
REFRESHING TEA
ETHERN BLACK TEA 1 TSP
LEMON 1/4 WEDGE
HONEY SAP 1 TSP
MARIAE CASTLE LUNCH
ESTERPIKE FIRE RADISHES 2 BULBS
PHEASANT MEAT 1 PORTION
STRAKTON YELLOW ROOT 1 ROOT
SALT & PEPPER DASH
OIL 1 TBSP
SALT BUN
FLOUR 1 CUP
SALT 1 TSP
YEAST 1/2 TSP
WATER 1/2 CUP

FIRST, TAKE THE ETHERN BLACK TEA AND STEEP IN HOT WATER. WAIT FOR 4 MINUTES. 5 MINUTES FOR A STRONGER TASTE. POUR OUT INTO A JUG. SQUEEZE AND STRAIN THE LEMONE WEDGE AND SET ASIDE. ADD HONEY SAP AND JUICE TO THE BLACK TEA AND COOL WITH LAKE ICE. SET ASIDE. CLEAN THE ESTERPIKE FIRE RADDISHES, REMOVE WILTED STEMS AND WASH THOROUGHLY. BRINE IN WATER. TAKE PHEASANT PORTION AND SALT. PUT ASIDE FOR 10 MINUTES. GRILL UNTIL DONE. PROOF YEAST IN WARM WATER. MAKE SURE NOT TO USE HOT WATER. TAKE FLOUR, PUT IN A BOWL AND MIX T HER. IT WILL START OUT CLUMPY BUT KEE T. KNEAD INTO A ROUGH BALL. FORM INT H BALL AND KNEAD TILL SMOOTH PUT I ED BOWL AND LET R
OH NO!
END

HURRY

SALVE
CLICK
ARM'S HURTING AGAIN?
JUST THE USUAL.
NOW, HURRY UP, WE'RE LATE TO THE MEETING.
YEAH, YEAH.

SAFETY
IT IS FOR THE SAFETY OF UNITY.
EVERY CAMBRIAN IN THE RANKS MUST BE DETAINED FOR NOW.
WHAT?
PLEASE UNDERS- TAND.
WE'RE LOYAL TO UNITY! OUR BLOOD AND ROOTS ARE HERE IN MARIAE.
THIS IS TEMPORARY WE APPREACIATE OUR CITIZEN'S COOPERATION.
BUT...
SIS?
W-WE'LL BE FINE. WHEN WE GET OUT...
...WHAT DO YOU WANT TO DO LATER?

PREPARING
LAUREL FOR VICTORY
ELENA,
ROSEMARY FOR REMEMBRANCE
I AM AFRAID
BUT NOW I AM READY

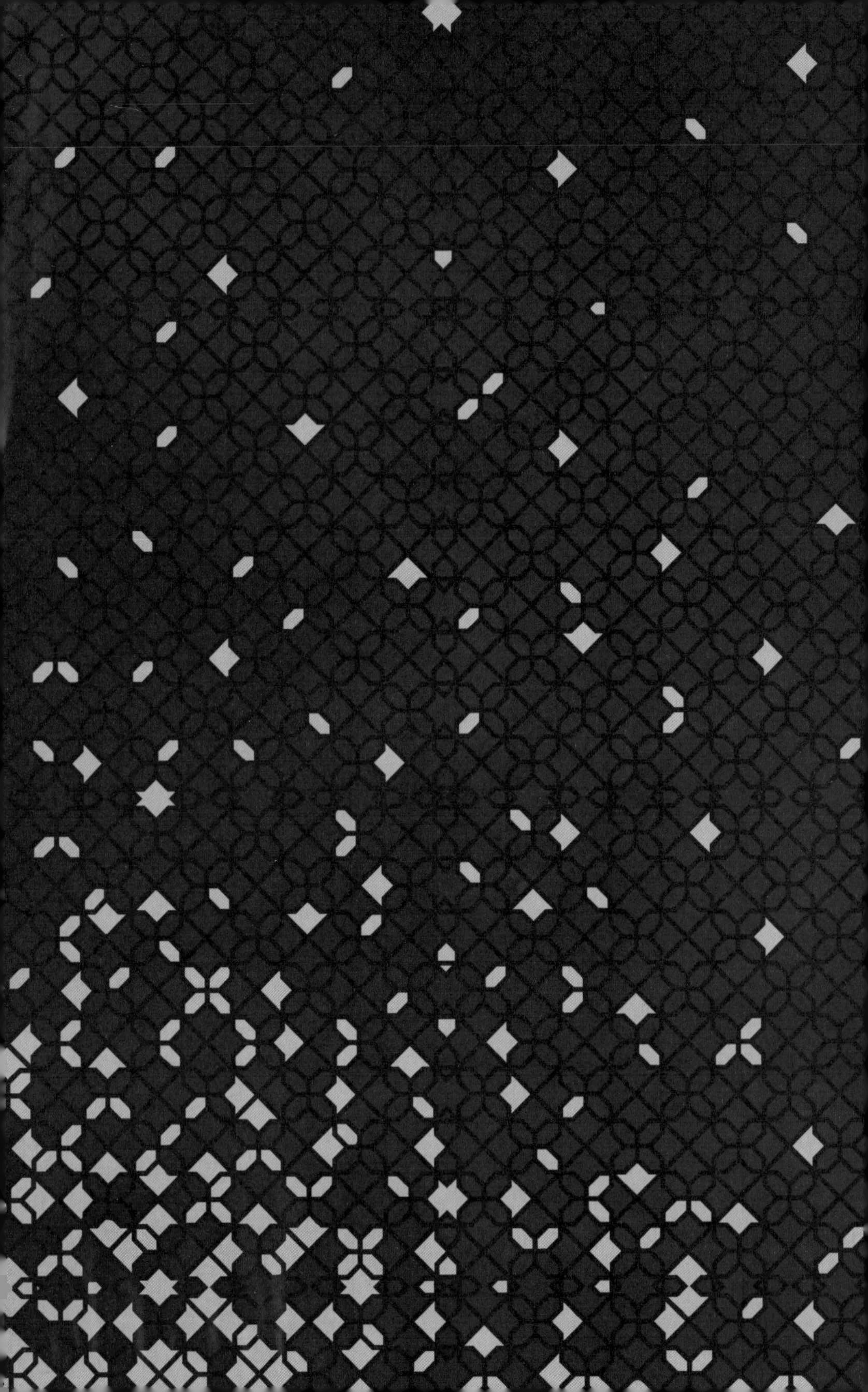